Specimen Sight-Reading Tests for Flute

Grades 6–8

ABRSM

GRADE 6

1

2

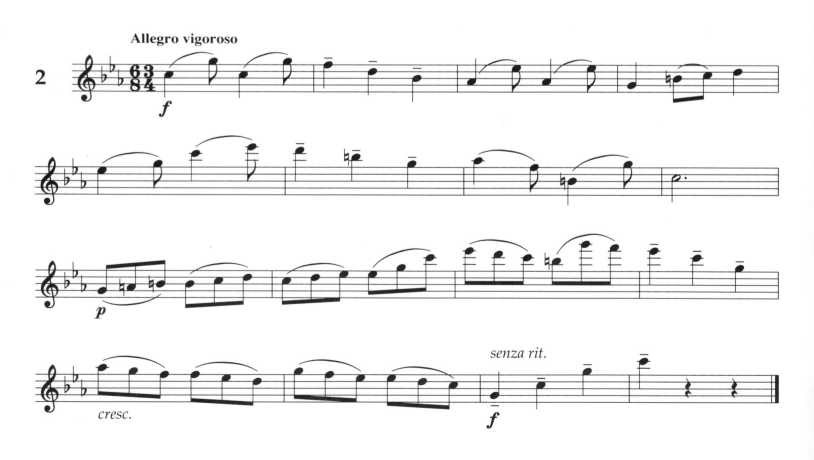

AB 2518

5

Allegro vigoroso

6

Andante

7 Adagio misterioso

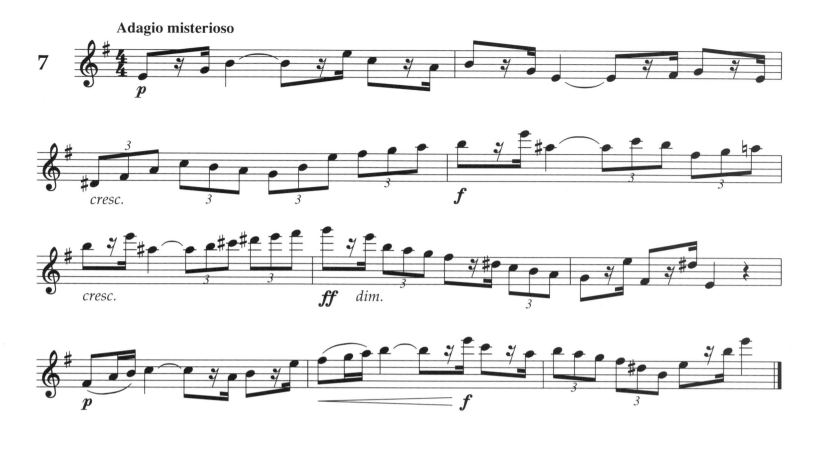

8 Con moto

Allegro ma non troppo

12

Brightly

13

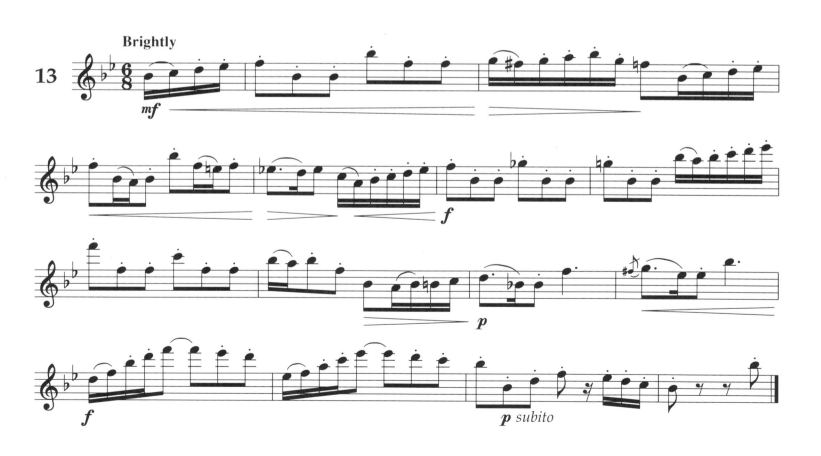

GRADE 7

5

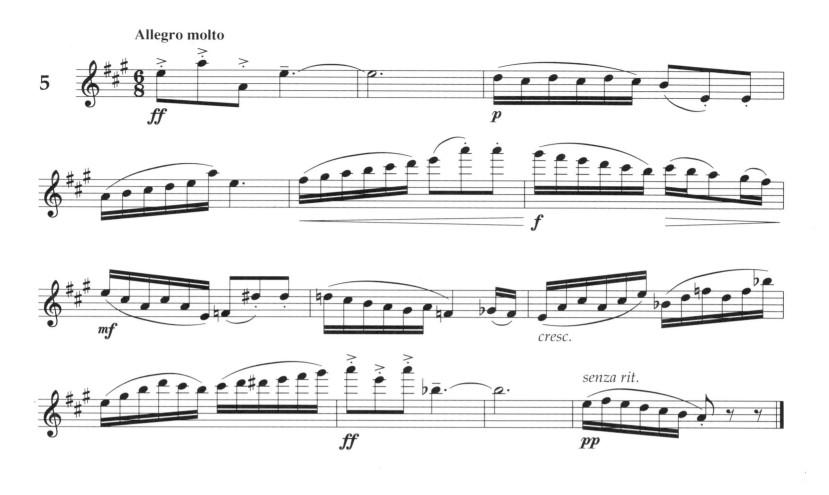

6 Lento espressivo

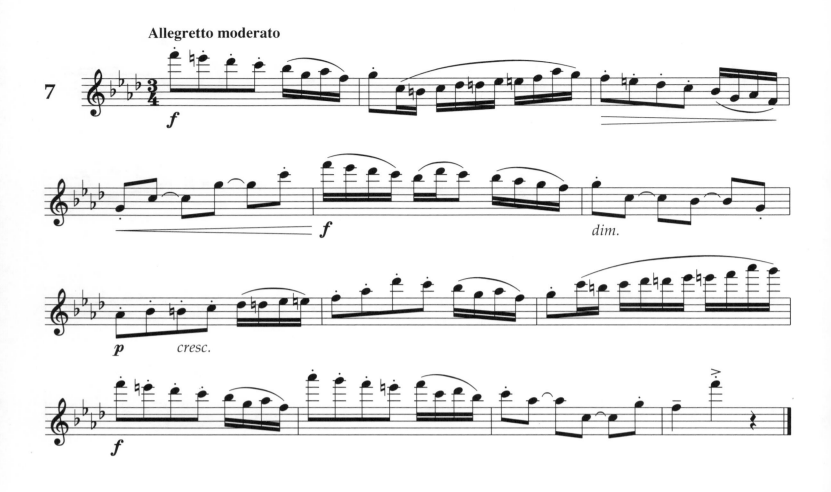

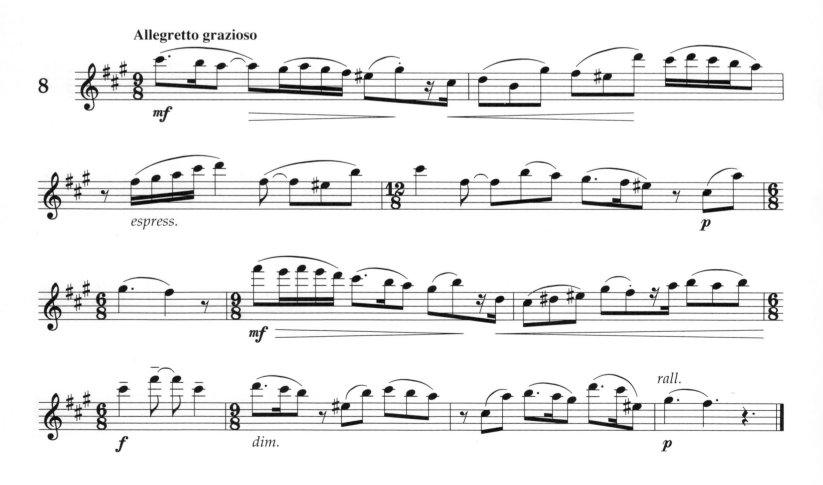

9

Maestoso

10

Andante misterioso

GRADE 8

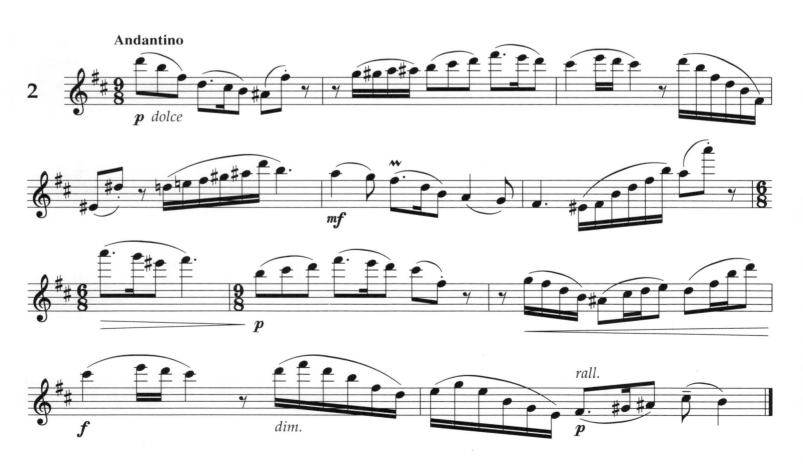

Allegretto con moto

Andante

AB 2518

Typeset by Musonix

Printed in England by Caligraving Limited Thetford Norfolk

10.10